Free A Fairy Tale Retelling of Rapunzel

The Crown and the Sceptre, Volume 0

Kristina J Jordan

Published by Kristina J Jordan, 2021.

FREE A FAIRY TALE RETELLING OF RAPUNZEL

First edition. June 12, 2021.

Copyright © 2021 Kristina J Jordan.

ISBN: 979-8201137496

Written by Kristina J Jordan.

CHAPTER 1

Avella closed her eyes tight, concentrating on her heartbeat. She had to slow it down. She just had to.

Thud. Thud. Thud.

She took a deep breath through her nose.

In. Out. In. Out.

The wild pounding of her heart slowed. She cracked her eyes open peering through the moonlight that splashed through the window. Hoping, wishing with all her might that tonight would be different. Her eyes drifted through the soft cocoon of darkness. Maybe everything would be all right. Maybe tonight would be different. A dim glow, crackling, breaking through the shadows; taunting her with orange flickering light.

With practiced speed, she reached for the bucket at her side and threw a cup of water over the licking flames. A small fire this time. But still fire—still dangerous. Avella swallowed back her fear; this was going to upset mother. She laid back down and closed her eyes; knowing that sleep would never come. It never did after one of her episodes. Drawing the covers up to her chin, Avella kept her eyes glued to the window, waiting for morning to break.

"Again?" Natalia's cold angry voice broke the silence.

"I'm sorry, mother. I was asleep. It just—happened," Avella kept her head down, eyes on the floor.

"You've been so difficult lately. Why can't you control it? The rest of us do. I never had this problem." Mother flicked her hand in disgust at the ruined book. A charred hole in the thick volume a reminder of last night's mishap.

"If you can't take care of your books, you just won't have them anymore. I'll have them moved to the library today."

Avella caught her breath. Books were her salvation; the only thing that took her away from her sister's resentment, her mother's anger, and father who didn't care.

"It's nearly time to go to court. This is Madelaine's most important year, you know that. Your sister's coming of age year. And yours will be next year; you need to make connections now; let them see your face. You are pretty, you know—in spite of... everything else. The duke of Vaseria's son will be in court this year, he's taking time away from his estate." Natalia pressed her lips together, annoyance marring her own beautiful face.

"Truly mother, I didn't even know the magic was happening until I woke up." Avella forced back the tears that clogged her throat.

"I know you're lying. It's impossible to do magic *this* powerful while sleeping. If people find out we can't control our magic, we'll be the laughingstock of everyone at court. I expect you to clean this up, then come down to breakfast immediately. And do go tidy your hair. It looks as if you were *trying* to turn it into a bird's nest."

Ignoring the woebegone look on her daughter's face, Natalie turned on her heel, closing the door with a firm click.

As the tapping footsteps faded down the hall, Avella scraped up the remnants of the mess, wiping down the desk until not a single flake of ash remained. Wrapping the destroyed book in an old cloth, she slipped down the hall, holding the offending item behind her back.

"What have you got behind your back?" Madelaine's perfect golden hair lay sleek against her head, not a wrinkle disturbed the ruffles of her pink dress. Acutely aware she was in her crumpled nightdress with her hair awry; Avella clutched her parcel tight behind her back in a foul mood. I should have known this was your fault." A look of disgust crossed Madelaine's face as her little dog, Coco, pranced through the ashes, getting soot on her snow-white paws. Madelaine shrieked.

"Look what you've done." She picked up the little dog, holding it away from her in both hands. "She's just had a bath yesterday afternoon."

Avella knelt down, snatching up the book and stuffing it back into its cloth wrapping. "I am trying, you know," she said in a low voice.

Madelaine tossed her hair, her grip firm on the wriggling dog. "Well, see that you get it sorted. I don't want your childish lack of control ruining my chances in my coming out year. And go brush your hair. You look a fright." She flounced toward the dining room, shouting for the maid to come wash the dog.

After disposing of the ruined book, Avella splashed water on her face and smoothed her hair before going down to breakfast. A bowl of congealed porridge marked her place at the table. She slid into her seat, wincing as the chair scraped loudly against the polished wooden floor. "Is that really necessary?" Her sister sniped. She patted her mouth with her napkin.

"Madelaine." Her mother's voice was calm, too calm. A clear sign she was unhappy about something. "Please remember, Madelaine, a lady is always kind. Even when other people are being difficult." She shot Avella a pointed glance.

Avella picked up her spoon and took a bite. The porridge was freezing; but she didn't dare complain. She took another bite, trying not to grimace as the gluey mixture slipped down her throat. Avella scanned the table for something to sweeten the bland substance, sighing. The honeypot had been scraped clean, Madelaine no doubt, she loved to slather it on her toast.

"Madelaine." Her mother's voice spoke sweetly. "Would you please speak to the housekeeper? Ask her what time we are to be at the dressmakers. I wouldn't want to be late for your appointment."

Madelaine huffed sweeping out of the room.

"You're coming to the dressmakers with us," Natalie informed Avella. "You're growing so fast you can't go to court looking like a scarecrow."

Avella nodded, forcing herself to take another bite.

"Good. Make sure you tidy yourself up before we leave." Natalie gave her daughter a disapproving look.

Half an hour later, Avella was climbing into the family carriage.

"I was thinking the midnight blue for an evening dress, darling. Perhaps in brocade." Natalie ignored Avella, directing her comments to Madelaine. "Something white for day...a nice organza or silk."

"Yes, mother." Madelaine stroked Coco, who was sitting on her knee. "And maybe if she has a lighter blue... it is a good color isn't it?"

Natalie pursed her lips, thinking. "That could work. We'll see. We can get more dresses, better ones, when we arrive in Florin. There will be much more of a selection in the city. I know the prince loves riding. We'll see about a really fabulous riding habit. You sit so well on a horse. It's the best place to stand out from the rest of the girls."

Avella turned her attention to the window, staring at the fluffy sheep scattered across the fields. They never included her in these conversations about fashion; but this had stopped bothering her a long time ago. If they had asked her, she would have had to inform Madelaine that white against her pale skin left her pasty and washed out. That would hardly be a pleasant conversation. Avella twisted her lips wryly at the thought.

The carriage rolled to a stop in front of the dressmakers; the footman opened the door; helping Natalie and the girls out of the carriage.

"We'll have to stop at the apothecary first; I need something for my nerves." Natalie shot a pointed glare at Avella. Avella lowered her head, following her mother and sister down the street. She enjoyed going to the apothecary. The soothing smell of eucalyptus and herbs from the tinctures and poultices, the long wooden counter with a bank of tiny drawers behind it. Each one filled with a different ingredient. She examined the rows of jars and bottles as they entered.

"Good morning, my lady." Althea, the healer, bustled to the front of the counter. A long white apron covered her dress, streaked with smears of salves and crumbs of ground up herbs.

Avella smiled. Althea was her favorite person in town. She was always kind and her soothing voice was nearly as good as her salves for making Avella feel better.

"Althea, thank goodness you're here." Natalie's fretting voice rang through the air. "I need some more of your tincture. The one for my nerves. And some lavender mixture. You know the one I use for the bath?"

Althea nodded politely. "Certainly, my lady. And anything for the girls?"

"Do you need anything, Madelaine?" Natalie turned to her daughter. "Do you have some of that soap? The one with the honey and arrowroot—is that the one you like, darling?"

"Yes, mother." Madelaine snuggled Coco close, stroking her head.

Althea gathered the items, wrapping them in crisp brown paper and tied it with twine. "And something for you—this is your favorite, isn't it?" She handed a small muslin-wrapped packet to Avella with a wink. Avella lifted the packet to her nose, breathing in the spicy floral scent.

"You shouldn't have, she doesn't need that." Natalie pursed her lips.

"It's no matter." Althea smiled.

With a huff, Madelaine and Natalie swept out of the apothecary. Avella clutched the wrapped package in her hand. Much as she appreciated the gesture, she knew her mother would hold it against her; most likely taking out her annoyance when she was least expecting it.

The door jingled as they entered the dressmakers. Bolts of fabrics lined the walls. Jewel like silks and satins, fine soft wools, and rows of colorful muslins. Avella drank it all in as the dressmaker led them to the settee and brought tea and biscuits. Natalie was by far the dressmaker's best customer; and they always received the royal treatment here.

Avella added three lumps of sugar in her tea and stirred, being careful not to let it slop over the edge of the cup. She would be here for a while; she let her eyes rove the tiny shop, watching idly as Natalie and Madelaine engaged in a lively debate about the merits of silk versus satin. Finally, Natalie decided, and the dressmaker began to pin the pattern on Natalie, who preened, lapping up every bit of attention.

Avella took another biscuit, enjoying the relative peace, broken only by the soft murmur of voices; when out of the corner of her eye, she saw a movement. It was not a mouse; it was a rat. A big horrible rat, with beady pink eyes and a long naked tail. The rat raised its nose, twitching its long gray whiskers as it sniffed the air.

Avella squeaked, spilling her tea over her lap. The rat peaked is head out from behind a bolt of yellow muslin, then darted forward, using scrabbly claws to scurry up the edge of her dress.

Avella shrieked, standing up and shaking out her dress. The dressmaker spun around, mouth full of pins. Just in time to see a large bolt of fabric explode into in a ball of fire.

"Avella stop!" her mother screamed.

Avella tried to calm down and slow her heartbeat, but it was too late. Another bolt of fire streaked out, catching the edge of the dressmaker's form on fire.

"Get her out of here," screeched Madelaine.

Natalie grabbed Avella by the arm, rushing her outside, just as the curtains went up in flames. Madelaine scooped up her little dog, and the dressmaker ran out behind them, narrowly missing being scorched by the inferno that had been her curtains.

"Avella, how could you?" Natalie shouted above the roar of the fire.

"I'm sorry, mother, I didn't mean to. I was just startled," Avella sobbed. A few quick-thinking villagers had by now gathered. One ran in with a bucket he had scooped from the watering trough and threw it on the curtains. Dousing the flames. Another bucket put out the other fire. Everything was a sodden mess, but they had saved the shop.

"Are you all right, miss?" a man asked with his hand on Avella's shoulder, his hazel eyes filled with concern. "My caravan is in front of the mercantile. If you want to sit down for a minute."

"She's fine," snapped Natalie, dismissing the kind man. Ignoring the fact that Avella's legs shook like jelly, she was shivering from head to toe.

"You're such an embarrassment." Natalie took Avella by the arm, her nails biting into her arm. "Come Madelaine, we'll have to return later; when we won't be interrupted."

Without so much as a backward glance, she dragged Avella away, leaving the smouldering mess behind. Madelaine followed, scooping up her little dog.

"But mother, what about my dresses?" Madelaine complained as the footman opened the door to the carriage.

"We'll send for the dressmaker to come to us. Don't worry, darling, I'll make sure you shine at court," Natalie soothed her eldest daughter.

Avella endured the ride back to the manor in silence. Madelaine sulked in the corner, and Natalie was seething with anger. Avella knew she would punish her when she got home. But how was the question.

The moment they arrived home, Natalie stomped to father's study; where Avella heard raised voices. She forced down the lump in her throat and headed upstairs to wait for her punishment. If she was very good—very quiet—Natalie might forget about the punishment. She curled up on the bed, trying to read a book.

Madelaine stood in the doorway, smirking.

Avella sighed, setting the book down; she wasn't reading it, anyway.

"Do you know what they're talking about in there?" Avella knew she shouldn't ask but couldn't help herself.

Madelaine sat on the edge of the bed. "Oh, it's the usual. Mother's having a fit, and father doesn't care, whatever is the least effort as usual. He told her to do whatever she wants to do—he knows she will, anyway."

Avella plucked at a loose thread on the coverlet. "I try to control it, I really do… it's just if I'm startled, I can't help it. Why did I have to be cursed with the gift?"

An odd expression flickered in Madelaine's eyes. "You're not the only one. It's just our gifts are different."

"Do you mean you…" Avella had no inkling that her sister had a gift as well.

"It's not like yours," Madelaine answered.

"Can you show me—how to use it?" Avella slid Madelaine a hopeful look.

Madelaine shook her head, "I don't think I can. Besides," she took Avella by the hand and led her to the vanity.

Avella followed. Madelaine pushed her down on the cushioned seat and leaned in next to her sister.

"Look at me and look at you," Madelaine told her.

Avella peered at their reflection in the mirror. It was obvious the girls were sisters. They shared the same golden hair, the straight nose, and the same clear eyes, gazed back at her.

"What am I supposed to be looking for?" she turned to her sister, confusion in her eyes.

"I can't let you come to court with me." Madelaine flipped her hair, twisting her lips. "The prince will take one look at you, then forget I exist."

Avella turned back to the mirror. "I doubt that's true." She turned back and forth, not seeing what Madelaine was talking about.

"That's why I had to make sure…" Madelaine continued. "That you wouldn't be there. And after today's stunt? Let's just say mother isn't thrilled about the idea of you coming to court with us." She pressed her lips together, her eyes hard.

"The rat… that was you?" Avella turned her incredulous gaze to her sister.

Madelaine shrugged, "I did what I had to do." She raised an eyebrow and stepped back from the mirror, fluffing her dress. "Make sure you comb your hair before you come down to dinner. You know what mother's like when you're untidy." With a swish of silk, she swept out, slamming the door behind her. At dinner, Avella cut her asparagus into tiny pieces, moving them around on her plate. Her food was long cold, and mother didn't like it when she didn't finish dinner, but she didn't know if she could swallow anything over the lump in her throat.

Across the table, Madelaine took a dainty bite, a satisfied smile on her face.

Natalie cleared her throat, then leaned forward. "Avella dear. I've been speaking with your father, and we've decided."

Avella set down her fork and wiped her sweating hands on her dress as she waited for them to mete out her punishment.

"About what, mother. If it's about what happened today, I really am so sorry. I will do better, I promise." Every muscle tensed as she waited for her mother's answer. Avella knew father had no control over this decision. She met Natalie's cold eyes... still waiting as Natalie dragged out the moment.

"We've decided that this year, you won't come to court for the season. It's too risky. What if you set something on fire? We'll reconsider next year; maybe you'll have learned a bit more... control by then. You understand, don't you? It would ruin everything for Madelaine," she tossed her eldest daughter a fond smile.

And for you. The thought swooped in before Avella could bat it away. She just *knew* her parents; no—her *mother* had ambitious plans at court. Plans to climb the social ladder. King Stephano and Queen Odilla had a son—a son who needed to marry and produce an heir. In spite of her pushing Madelaine toward Ruben, the Duke's son; Avella suspected that if Madelaine didn't get fobbed off on the prince, she would. She shivered, remembering his cold, flat eyes that sent chills up her spine every time they met. There was something off about the Prince. But that would never stop her mother.

"...with your grandmother."

Avella jerked to a stop, fork clattering to the plate. "Grandmother?" her eyes widened. Her father's mother, a warm soft woman, was long gone. Glandular fever claimed her when Avella was in her tenth year. The other grandmother—her mother's mother—had never been mentioned in her presence. Avella always assumed she was dead as well.

"With whom?" she repeated, thinking maybe she heard the name wrong.

"Don't gape like that, darling. It isn't attractive. We're sending you to your grandmother for the season. She can help you with your...problem." Natalie stirred cream into her tea.

Avella snapped her mouth shut.

"So that's settled then. You may start your packing after dinner. Tonight. We'll be very busy getting Madelaine ready for the season. You wouldn't want to be underfoot and hurt your sister's chance of a suitable match now, would you?" Leaving no room to argue, her mother rang the bell, signalling for the plates to be taken away.

Alone at the table, Avella pushed her dinner away. The only bright spot was she didn't have to eat the full plate of food. Her stomach lurched as she mulled over this recent development. *Maybe my grandmother is really lovely.* Avella set down her napkin and pushed her plate away. It could be pleas*ant—she closed her eyes, imagining a cozy woman doing needlepoint in a rocking chair.*

Avella left the table and went to the garden; her favorite place to think. She sat on a wrought-iron bench, gazing idly at the ducks swimming across the pond. Out of the corner of her eye, she watched Madelaine. Her little dog was prancing at her side. Madelaine held out a hand, and a robin flew down and perched on her finger, chirping in delight. Avella sighed. *Why couldn't I have a pretty gift like Madelaine did?* Avella thought to herself. Animals always loved Madelaine, flocking to her. Even the grumpy badger in the back garden followed Madelaine like a devoted puppy. She turned back to the house. If she didn't start her packing, who knows what her mother would do to her next.

Avella's dreams of a cozy relationship with her grandmother were dashed the moment the woman stalked into the house. Refusing to even sit and have a cup of tea, she stood stiffly at the door, waiting impatiently for Avella to fasten her cloak.

"Thank you for doing this mother." Natalie joined her mother in the hall, her usually poised expression hesitant, even fearful. Avella's heart clenched tight in her chest, wondering what it meant when someone could intimidate even the unflappable Natalie.

"I'll soon have the matter sorted out," Sorchia swept her eyes across Avella, taking in the slightly messy golden hair and untied laces on her boots. "Hurry, we don't have all day." She tapped her gloved fingers together.

"We'll come for you when we get back, darling." The familiar scent of her mother's expensive perfume enveloped her as she brushed cool lips against her cheek. "Behave and make sure you do everything your grandmother tells you."

"She can call me Sorchia; grandmother won't be necessary." Her grandmother's raspy voice grated through the air. "And don't worry, I'll see that she behaves."

When they loaded the last trunk in the carriage, they were off. Clattering down the drive in the rumbling carriage. Avella turned, taking one last look out the back window as the manor house faded from her view. Little did Avella realize she would never be home again.

CHAPTER 2

"I hear you've been causing mischief," her grandmother pinned her with cold eyes.

Avella lowered her eyes, staring at the cracks in the floor of the carriage. "I try not to." Her voice was small and weak.

"See that you don't." Sorchia pursed her lips and turned to the window, fingering a worn book in her hand.

Silenced, Avella let her eyes wander around the carriage. It was clear the decrepit carriage was once grand, but the faded gold leaf design and worn velvet seats told her it had seen better days. A musty smell drifted up from the cushions. Grandmother must not travel much.

"We're here." The stern voice broke into her thoughts.

"Already?" Surprised, Avella jerked her head up. They had barely left the estate. The carriage squeezed down a narrow lane so overgrown with brambles that Avella had to shrink back from the windows to avoid being scraped by thorny stems. The carriage stopped in front of a crumbling manor house, and Sorchia stepped down.

"Well. Are you coming?" Sorchia turned, an irritable expression on her patrician features.

Taken aback by the impatient tone, Avella quickly scrambled out of the carriage, nearly tripping over still untied laces as she followed Sorchia up the stone steps. The front door swung open on creaky hinges, Avella blinked, adjusting to the dim interior after the bright sunlight. She followed her grandmother up three flights of stairs until they reached a tiny attic room. The simple room contained a row of pegs on the wall and one small cupboard next to the narrow bed. Avella wondered how she was to fit all her dresses in the small space, but her grandmother's raspy voice quickly corralled her wandering thoughts.

"Come downstairs as soon as you get washed. We can talk while I have my tea," Sorchia shut the door behind her with a firm click. Avella sank on the narrow bed and concentrated on her breathing. Her heart beat quickened, and if she didn't get it under control, something was going to happen. Something bad.

In. Out. In. Out.

She breathed the words through her mouth and nose. Gradually, her heart slowed to an even pace. She cracked her eyes open cautiously. Then, bang. A loose shutter slapped against the window, startling Avella. Before she could calm herself, a spark shot across the room, lighting the curtains on fire. Avella jumped up, tearing the fabric from the window and bundling it to the floor, until only a wisp of smoke remained.

"Is everything all right in there?" Sorchia's rigid figure stood in the doorway, eyes hard.

"Yes, grandmother," Avella put her hands behind her back.

"If everything is all right, what happened to my curtains?" her grandmother's sharp eyes settled on the empty window frame.

"Um... there was an accident." Avella bowed her head, waiting for the tirade to begin.

Sorchia took one step across the room and backhanded Avella, snapping her head against the wall. Blinking back the stinging tears in her eyes, Avella put her hand to her cheek. In spite of thoughtlessness that verged on cruelty, her mother and father had never laid a hand on her. She took a deep breath to still her racing pulse. Calm yourself before it's too late, she scolded herself. But it was too late.

This time, it wasn't a stray spark that flew out, a ball of fire that shot across the room, only missing Sorchia by a narrow margin before it landed in the hallway, scorching a black circle onto the polished wooden floor before fizzling out.

Sorchia raised thin eyebrows. "So that's what your mother was hiding. I wondered why she suddenly asked for my assistance after all these years. Well, don't worry, child, this is something I can help you with."

"You can?" Although her cheek still burned red with her grandmother's handprint, Avella felt a new sensation stir deep inside. Hope.

"Yes. Of course. It might take some time; perhaps a minor sacrifice or two. But if you're willing, I can teach you." Her grandmother's eyes gleamed with a strange light. "Now, come down for tea. I'll send someone up to clean that and mend the curtains later." She stepped over the blackened floorboards and down the hall, the acrid smell of smoke drifting after her.

"Now tell me," grandmother stirred a cup of tea, swirling the liquid before adding a splash of milk. "What exactly does it feel like when this happens—the fire?"

Avella sat on the edge of a faded damask chair with her hands folded neatly in her lap. "It happens when I get excited, my heart beats really fast, and then, it just builds until it explodes out of me."

To Avella's surprise, her grandmother laughed, a bitter grating sound, as if out of practice. "I'm sure it quite surprised Natalie to discover the gift jumped right past her and settled on you, her youngest daughter."

"The gift?" This was a new concept to Avella, who had been taught her strange power was more of a curse than a gift.

"Yes. Gift." The Rapunzel family has always been gifted. Passed down through the daughters until your mother came along. An expression of distaste crossed her features. "It's her common blood. Her father didn't have much of a bloodline."

Avella sneaked a cautious glance at the older woman, wondering what her grandmother's gift might be. "You need to learn to control and use the gift. If you can control it, the world will be ours."

"That's the problem," Avella looked away as she twisted her hands together in her lap. "I *can't* control the gift; I just get excited and it happens. I try to breathe slowly, but that only works sometimes." She bit her lip.

"Ahh... but you're thinking about this backwards. You need to learn how to manipulate the gift—not eradicate *it*. Train it to do your bidding. Instead of stopping it, learn how to bring it out when you need it. With gifts come power," Sorchia smiled as she fingered the small book in her lap.

Avella pushed back her thick honey colored hair to glance around the room, taking in the ragged furnishings and peeling wallpaper. Her grandmother's gift didn't appear to have done much service to her fortunes. The once grand manor was shabby.

"I see that look on your face. Unfortunately, even the best plans sometimes go astray. But you, my dear. You and I—we are going to change all that." She took a sip of tea, a rigid smile on her face.

CHAPTER 3

Avella looked out into the sun-soaked garden, smelling the fresh earth. In spite of the run-down condition of the manor house; the garden was magnificent. Even in winter, it somehow managed to be a riot of lush green interspersed with splashes of brightly colored flower. Curious, because in the few weeks she had spent here, she hadn't seen a single gardener. She watched the rigid form of her grandmother striding across the lawn. She stopped, her black dress a stain against the bright green grass; then raised both hands in the air. A wind blew, whipping her grandmother's long black skirts around her legs. Then she saw it. Tendrils of green, pushing their way up through the grass, creeping around her Sorchia, like her pets—and maybe they were. Shocked, Avella let the curtains fall shut as she turned away from the window. So, this is what her grandmother's gift was, she could make things grow. She wondered what had made her grandmother a pariah. Almost a ghost. No one at court had ever mentioned her. Not once. And certainly, never at home either. Avella pondered the mystery as she sat at a writing table.

"Hello dear, I've brought you some tea." Sorchia rapped at the door, carrying a tray with tea and cakes. Avella took the cup, grateful for its heat. In spite of the fire burning, the manor house was always chilly.

Grandmother took a seat by the fireplace, watching as Avella sipped her tea. Bitter, but she didn't like to complain; she took another sip. Over the past two weeks, Sorchia had been civil, almost kind at times. Not kind, but civil. They didn't speak of the time she had struck her, but

Sorchia didn't seem likely to do it again, so Avella decided not to bring it up again.

"Do you like it?" Sorchia's voice broke the silence. "That tea is my special recipe."

"Delicious." Avella forced down another gulp. She felt lightheaded and strange, almost as if something were crawling under her skin. She took another gulp of the tea before setting it aside.

"I thought we could do a little training today. I want to see what you're capable of," Sorchia stood up, gesturing for Avella to follow. She led her through the kitchen to an empty courtyard behind the manor. "You won't be able to hurt anything here," Sorchia explained, gesturing toward the worn brick walls.

Avella nodded, her head was aching, and instead of going away, the strange feeling was intensifying. A buzzing noise sounded in her ears, faint at first, but growing louder and more persistent.

Sorchia pointed to a mark drawn on the brick wall across the courtyard. "I want you to see if you can hit that."

"With fire?" her grandmother had gone for two weeks without bringing up the incident. Surprisingly, the fires had stopped. Completely. Each night passed peacefully, and Avella hoped that her unfortunate episodes would become a distant memory.

"Of course, with fire." An impatient look crossed Sorchia's face, startling Avella.

Avella had never *purpose*fully created fire before, and she didn't know where to start. She squeezed her eyes tight, willing that familiar frantic feeling, the speeding pulse. Nothing happened. There was no rapid heartbeat, no panic welling up in her chest. She opened her eyes peeking at her grandmother who stood ramrod straight staring at her with an expression of distaste.

"Well, come on now," Sorchia tapped her booted foot.

Avella squeezed her eyes shut and tried again, but she couldn't replicate that feeling, that strange tingling that buzzed through her veins before the sparks would emerge. "I... I don't know how." She studied her feet, wilting under the haughty glare.

Grandmother huffed, "I suppose, you may need a bit of a crutch." She reached behind her and drew out a long switch, a thin piece of reed. Avella hadn't noticed it leaning against the wall. Sorchia rapped it against her hand, a grim expression lurking in her eyes. Avella stared in shock. Was her grandmother actually intending on hitting her with that? She closed her eyes again, embracing the jolt of panic as fear raced through her veins. There. A tiny flash ignited, then fizzled out, leaving a tiny mark on the ground in front of her.

"You need to do better than that," grandmother took a step toward her, raising the switch ever so slightly as she flicked it in the air.

This time, the threat worked. A fist sized ball of flame smacked against the stone wall, nowhere near the mark on the wall, but it left a constellation of ash behind it. Ash rained down in a fine mist around them, dusting their hair with flecks of soot.

"Better," grandmother lowered the switch. Avella rubbed her eyes, the ache was building into a full-blown headache, dark spots swam before her eyes, making her dizzy.

"Can I go inside now? I don't' feel very well," Avella's voice was small.

"No, not until you get this right. Try again, this time with more accuracy." Sorchia drew her lips into a thin line.

After hours of practice, Avella's legs were like jelly. She could barely see through the pain lancing through her head. She had avoided her grandmother's switch so far; but she suspected from the look in Sorchia's eyes she wouldn't hesitate to use it if got her the result she wanted.

"I suppose that will do for now." Much to Avella's relief, Sorchia set the switch down.

Avella leaned against the wall, spent.

"We'll start again tomorrow," Sorchia spun on her heel and left Avella alone in the courtyard.

In Sorchia's small realm, each day followed the same predictable routine. Breakfast followed by that strange cup of bitter tea before a gruelling practice session. In spite of the unpleasantness of the practice, Avella found it easier and easier to pull on the energy that fuelled her strange gift. Soon she was creating enormous balls of fire, flinging them with such accuracy that she could aim them through the branches of a tree without singing a single leaf. Best of all—no more fires. Avella slept so soundly each night; never stirring from the moment her head hit the pillow until morning.

"You're nearly ready," grandmother gave her a rare approving smile as she shot a tiny ball of fire through a crack in the courtyard wall.

"Ready for what?" Avella realized she had given no thought to the motivation behind her grandmother's training.

"Ready for court," grandmother fingered the pages of her little book. "That is what you wanted, isn't it—to show your mother and sisters you belong?"

"My coming out isn't until next year." Not fond of the rigid court protocols, not to mention the constant vying for position, Avella was more than content to wait another year. Besides, this was her sister's coming out year. Her mother would no doubt be on high alert for any perceived failures on her part. At least at her grandmother's there was some small measure of freedom.

Sorchia pursed her lips, a warning that she wasn't happy about something. "Well, I suppose we could go...." Avella quickly backtracked. "But I don't think mother got my things ready for court this year."

"Good," her grandmother gave a nod. "Let me worry about the dresses. We need to prepare. You may meet me in the study after you tidy yourself up." She ran her eyes over Avella's untidy hair before sweeping back into the house.

Avella brushed her thick golden hair and splashed cold water on her face before she tiptoed into her grandmother's study, seating herself in a high-backed chair across from Sorchia.

"You wanted to speak to me?" her voice was timid.

Sorchia threaded her fingers together and leaned back in her chair. "I was like you once. Young. Pretty. Naïve."

"I'm not…"

"Yes, you are. Untidy maybe, but beautiful; why do you think your sister is so jealous of you?" Sorchia's voice was sharp. "But this story isn't about you. It's about me. I was the toast of the court in my coming out year, I had my pick of all the suitors; but there was only one I wanted. The prince, he was handsome, dashing, and very, very much in love with me." Her face softened for a mere second, as she let the memories take her back.

Avella waited for her grandmother to continue.

"I had my power by then. In case you haven't noticed, I can make things grow. This only attracted the prince even more. He was no fool. Who wouldn't want power like mine running through the veins of their royal heirs? Power is everything in Iasia—don't you forget that. But, when you have that much attention; people get jealous, things happen. It started slowly. Silly rumors here and there that always proved to be untrue. And the prince was loyal to me. So loyal." Her stony face took on a proud expression.

Mesmerised, Avella kept her eyes glued to her grandmother's face as she relived her past.

"It was his sister-in-law who did it. The prince had a younger brother who married before him. She was pretty, too, but cunning. And jealous. She settled for Prince Cecile, his younger brother, because Prince Killian was her first choice, but he didn't want her. You can imagine how angry she was when he fell head over heels for me the year after he turned her down." A proud smile crossed her face, and Avella saw a hint of the beauty she must have possessed.

"What did she do?" Mesmerised, Avella imagined what her grandmother must have been like as a young girl. Before the harsh realities of life and lies had hardened her.

"Poison. She used castor beans to the best of my knowledge; then she told everyone she saw *me* do it. Of course, I hadn't kept my powers a secret...why should I? I had nothing to hide. Although no one could prove it, they all know I was capable of making the poison. There was a trial—an ugly one. My mother and father dropped me and would have anything to do with me anymore—they told me I brought shame to the family. So that was it. Oh, I eventually married, not to anyone in the nobility, none of them wanted to be associated to the scandal. I married a merchant. He didn't love me, but he knew I was an only child. In our family, the estate is like the gift—passed down through the daughters. Eventually I inherited the manor and the estate, I raised your mother here."

Sorchia rubbed her finger on the cover of her book, eyes tight with bitter thoughts.

"I've been waiting years for this opportunity—this moment," her eyes met Avella's, their coldness sent a shiver down her spine. "And you're the one who will to help me get my revenge. Your mother kept her family ties a secret; she's ashamed of where she came from. Too ashamed of me. No one knows about your abilities and what you can do. You can go to court freely... do anything you want."

The hairs on the back of Avella's neck prickled. Was her grandmother insinuating she should... her thoughts trailed off.

"As long as you keep drinking the tea I make, you'll be able to control the abilities. No one will ever suspect it was you—except maybe your mother and your sister, *they* would say nothing, they've worked too hard to get where they are. Do it somewhere public. Everyone will think it's an unfortunate accident. A candle tipping... a lantern that got too hot. You're a smart girl; you'll think of something." Sorchia's eyes glittered with satisfaction.

Avella's entire body stiffened as utter horror enveloped her. As much as she wanted to please her grandmother—or rather avoid *displeasing* her grandmother, this was a line she couldn't cross. She clenched her hands together; knuckles turning white with fear.

"Oh, I see that look on your face," Sorchia leaned forward, that irritable expression crossing her face. "Your morals are getting in the way, aren't they? Is it *such* a terrible thing to rid the world of evil? The woman is a cold-blooded killer. Who knows how many people she's harmed since—who's had to suffer at her hands? You know your mother has had her eye on the prince, if not for your sister then for you? Do you want someone like her as a family member? She would be your mother-in-law; you would be at her mercy."

"I just don't think...I mean..." Avella searched for words but found none. How could there be? Her own grandmother was asking her to take someone else's life.

"Do you need a bit more time to think about it, my dear?" Sorchia's eyes searched hers, stripping her soul bared with their intensity.

Avella grasped the opportunity to escape. She could plan what to say to Sorchia later. "Yes, grandmother," she lowered her eyes, uncomfortable knowing that eventually she would have to answer to her grandmother—and she would not be pleased with her.

"I understand, it's a big decision, and a risk on your part obviously. Now, drink your tea darling, you wouldn't want it to get cold." Avella took a sip of the bitter drink, wincing as the liquid slid down her throat. Moments later, she knew that was her biggest mistake. Her eyes grew heavy as they drooped and the room spun around her, colors swirling together like stained glass. The last thing she remembered before it all went black was her grandmother's iron grip on her arm, and the harsh whisper in her ear.

"I'm sorry, dear, but I can't let you go out spreading rumors around; I've waited too long to risk you ruining this for me. I'll take you to a safe place until you can see some sense."

The next few hours were a blur. Avella only remembered snippets; a vague recollection of being in a carriage, then lurching up a winding staircase. A thudding mallet was the last sound Avella remembered hearing. Then everything faded to black. Then it was morning.

CHAPTER 4

The sun streamed through the window, harsh against swollen eyes. Avella blinked, *where am I?* She wondered, stumbling out of a narrow cot. Stone walls surrounded her on every side. It appeared to be a small round room—a tower? She ran to the single window and looked over the sill. Thick trees surrounded her in every direction. She was high. Avella peered through their branches, looking for a landmark, but saw nothing; next she ran to the door, tugging at the handle with all her might, but Sorchia had locked it—or nailed shut and wouldn't budge.

Her eyes flickered around the room, she searched for anything that might help her escape; but the room contained very little. A pitcher of water, a loaf, and a lump of cheese. In the corner of the room stood a metal bucket. Avella turned away in disgust. Whoever put her up here must mean for her stay. Avella shivered with the cold, then wrapped the quilt around her shoulders, approaching the window. Maybe she could tie pieces of the quilt together and use them as rope and climb down the side of the tower. But to her dismay the quilt was far too thick to rip, and she was too high for it to reach the ground anyway. She would just have to wait, Avella sat on the bed wondering how long her grandmother planned to leave her here. Surely, she would check on her at some point; at least to give her food and water.

She waited. And waited. And waited. Morning turned to afternoon, then evening. Avella eventually ate a chunk of the bread and some cheese, being careful to save some food for later, and drank some water—water liberally sprinkled with Sorchia's herb mixture. She felt the bitter taste coated the back of her throat as she forced herself to swallow. She curled up on the bed again, finally falling into a restless sleep. It was well past noon the next day before she heard a human voice.

Avella ran to the window. "Grandmother, you came," she cried, so delighted to see someone, anyone, that would break up the monotony of the bare stone walls.

Sorchia stood at the bottom of the tower, rigid and stiff as she gazed up at Avella. "Have you done any thinking yet?"

Avella had done nothing but think since her grandmother had left her there. In doing so she realized a lot of things. The most important conclusion was she couldn't spend her life fulfilling the expectations of other people. People who would never be satisfied. She stiffened her spine, dreading her grandmother's reaction as she fought to keep her voice steady. "I have."

"Well?" Sorchia's cold eyes glared from the bottom of the tower.

"I will help you, grandmother, but only if you find another way. I just can't do... that." Avella trembled, knowing her grandmother's capability for rage.

"This *is* the only way," Sorchia spit out the words.

"I'm sorry grandmother, I will help you, just not like that." Avella locked eyes with her grandmother, an unfamiliar sense of determination and grit arose in her soul.

"Fine, if that's what you want." Sorchia took a step back, voice calm. Too calm. She set down the basket she was carrying, and drew out her little book, flicking through the worn pages, she ran her finger over the script, then closed her eyes. "Grow," she commanded, her eyes fierce and cruel.

A strange tingling sensation wrapped around Avella, settling on the top of her head. Then a prickling, stinging sensation that turned into an inferno of pain. She put her hands to her head, then gazed down in shock. Her hair was growing. Thick, honey-colored waves. In a mere instant they reached her feet then coiled, snakelike as they crept out the window sliding over the side of the stone tower. Avella stepped back, tugging at the hair as she tried to pull it back in the window, but the magic was relentless. In a few seconds, it reached the ground. The hair was heavy, so heavy. Avella struggled to keep her head upright against its weight.

"Now, hold still," Sorchia commanded. Before Avella could blink, she was climbing up the side of the crumbling wall, using Avella's newly grown hair like a rope. Tears stung Avella's eyes; it felt like her scalp was being ripped from her head. With inhuman speed, Sorchia reached the top and climbed in the window. She filled Avella's water pitcher, sprinkling a few of her mysterious herbs on top of the water, then set down another loaf of bread and some cheese.

"I see you're not ready to be reasonable yet. But you will be." Sorchia paced the room, pausing to rattle the door, ensuring it was still locked tight. "I'll be back to check on you." She climbed back out the window, gripping the hair as she swung her leg over the sill. When she reached the bottom, she looked up.

"Shrink," she commanded, opening the little book again. As quickly as it had grown, the hair shrank back into Avella's head, whipping itself back through the window. Still numb from shock, Avella watched as Sorchia left, disappearing silently into the thick foliage.

That was the new pattern. Sorchia came every few days, climbed up, delivered food and water, always with the herbs—herbs that dulled Avella's senses but left her with raging headaches. Before climbing out the window, Sorchia always tested the waters; asking the same question. Was Avella ready to reconsider.

Avella dreaded and looked forward to Sorchia's visits in equal measure. The loneliness overpowered her, her only company was the birds that swooped past her window and built their nests in the nearby trees. Her stomach was constantly growling. Sorchia never brought enough food; and her skin was itching because there wasn't enough water to wash in. At times she grew so distressed by the constant monotony and hunger she imagined what it would be like to give in to her grandmother's demands. It would be easy to agree, only one tiny moment. Avella could spend the rest of her life in atonement. But no, she reminded herself every time her thoughts strayed in that direction, some actions had no atonement. Her grandmother would give up, eventually; she had to.

One afternoon, everything changed. Avella was sitting by on the windowsill, watching a bluebird flit back and forth; wishing she had Madelaine's ability to coax it to her. Her grandmother was due to arrive any moment, she had eaten the last of her bread for breakfast; sprinkling the crumbs for the birds, hoping to entice them to the windowsill. She was hungry.

"Clover. Cloverrrr..." a voice, faint, but getting closer called. Avella leaned out the window as far as she could go, searching the trees, excitement pounding in her chest.

"Hello," Avella shouted down and a figure emerged from the edge of the clearing. Her heart thudded against her ribcage as she realized this might be the chance she had been waiting for.

The figure stopped short in surprise, then looked up. Hazel eyes framed by long lashes and a thatch of dark brown hair met hers.

"Hello miss." The boy—or young man, rather—smiled up at her, sweeping his cap into his hand. "I wasn't expecting to meet anyone here. Have you seen my dog? Brown, about this high, probably chasing after a rabbit."

"No. I haven't," Avella admitted. "And I've been sitting here all afternoon."

"What exactly are you doing up there?" the young man shaded his eyes as he craned his neck.

"I'm trapped. Do you think you could help me get down?" Avella answered, avoiding the question.

"Of course, my lady, I'll try the door." He disappeared from sight, then reappeared a moment later. "The door's locked, if you throw me the key, I'll try to open it from this side."

"I don't have a key," Avella admitted. "Someone locked me in here."

Concern flared in the strange man's eyes. "I have some tools in my caravan, I might be able to pry it open."

"Yes, please. But can you hurry? I don't know when she's coming back. And be careful. Don't let my grandmother see you; she's a lot more dangerous than you might think."

"I'll make sure of it." The stranger disappeared into the trees at a run. Avella kept her eyes glued to the spot he disappeared from, hardly daring to breathe as she waited for him to return. Much to her relief, he returned a few minutes later, tools in hand.

"I can probably pry these hinges off; they're thick though, it might take some time." He worked on the door, straining as he wedged a thin piece of metal against the hinges.

Avella kept her eyes glued to the spot Sorchia usually emerged from, watching for any movement in the trees.

"Stop," she whispered, when the branches rustled and moved. "Hide. I think she's coming."

Without a word, he slid around the side of the tower, taking his chisel with him. Avella pasted a placid expression on her face as Sorchia emerged from the trees with a basket on her arm. She stood in front of the tower, taking out the familiar little book.

"Grow," she commanded.

That familiar tingling danced across her scalp, as Avella's hair lengthened, twisting its way down the side of the tower. Then the excruciating, yanking, and pulling as her grandmother climbed up. No matter how many times it happened, Avella couldn't get used to this part of the process.

"What's wrong, dear? You look flushed." Sorchia placed her stiff fingers on Avella's forehead. Avella forced herself to breathe slowly.

"No grandmother, I'm fine, it's just a very hot day that's all."

"Have you had any time to think?" Sorchia moved over to the pitcher, pouring in some water, and sprinkling in her herbs.

"Yes, I have grandmother. But my answer is still the same." Avella met her grandmother's narrowed eyes.

"That's too bad. It's getting so very inconvenient coming here every day. I'm not as young as I once was, you know." In a huff, Sorchia set down the bread and cheese—an even smaller portion than usual—Avella noted, before climbing down.

"Shrink." Sorchia watched until the golden hair was just below Avella's shoulders, then turned to go. Just as she was about to leave, something caught her eye. She stalked over to the door, examining the frame carefully before turning to Avella.

"What is the meaning of this?" Sorchia pointed out a scrape on the weathered door. A scar of pale wood not yet exposed to the elements.

"I'm not sure." Avella widened her eyes innocently. "I heard some noises last night. I think it was an animal. Maybe a bear? Something with claws. I figured I'm too high for them. Can they?" she held her breath, hoping her grandmother would take the bait.

Sorchia examined the marks on the door suspiciously; not convinced. Abruptly, she turned, prowling the area, looking at the ground and muttering to herself.

"What is it, grandmother?" Avella desperately hoped the man had enough sense to hide while she occupied Sorchia inside the tower.

"Someone was here." Sorchia threw Avella an accusing look. And when I find them, there will be consequences. Consequences you won't like." Avella shrank back under her wrathful gaze.

After a few tense moments, Sorchia left, muttering something about a guard.

"Is it safe to come out now?" The man's voice came from nearby somewhere eye level. Avella started, nearly falling out the window.

"Where are you?" she craned her neck.

"Here. In the oak tree." There, clinging to the spreading branches, was the strange man.

"You stayed?" Avella's face brightened.

"Of course, I stayed. It wouldn't be right to leave you here; not with that witch." He hopped down from the lowest branch. "Let's get you out of here."

"All right, but we have to hurry. She knows you were here, and I heard her talking about a guard."

Getting Avella down from the tower proved to be an arduous task. Very difficult. The tools Pierre had didn't hold up to the task. The wood was too thick, and the iron fittings were too sturdy.

"I could get more tools in town." Pierre sat on the ground to rest.

"I guess so." Avella felt prospect of freedom, so close she could almost taste it, slip further and further away.

Pierre glanced at Avella and saw the woebegone look on her face. "It would take a few days. How often does she come back—I'd hate to come back only to find she's taken you away somewhere else." He patted Clover, his big shaggy dog who had wandered out of the woods not five minutes after Sorchia had disappeared down the path.

"Do you think she really would?" Avella's heart sank.

"She definitely *suspects*. And I heard her muttering about a guard; although I doubt that she'll trust anyone enough to come guard a helpless girl in an old tower. Her only choice is to move you or come back more frequently. It's going to be risky either way." Pierre glanced at the door, now bearing even more obvious marks of his efforts. In his efforts, he had scattered wood shavings and tools around the base of the tower.

"Usually she just comes every other day, sometimes every day. She likes to keep me on my toes." Avella leaned out the window. Usually shy, she surprised even herself by how comfortable she felt with this stranger. "I don't think she has anyone she could use as a guard, though. There are servants at the manor; but no one she trusts."

Pierre scratched his cheek, thinking for a moment. "What if you had the book she uses, do you think you could use it?"

"I don't know, I guess it's possible. We do share the same blood—but we have different gifts." Avella explained as she tilted her head thoughtfully. "But I suppose if I had the book, it means she can't use it to come up the tower anymore." Avella wondered why she had never thought of this before.

"If you take her book, I'll help you down from the tower the next time your grandmother comes." Pierre's hazel eyes brightened as he shared his plan with Avella.

Avella agreed. That night, she carefully scraped the herbs off the top of the water, removing every visible crumb. Whatever came next, she knew she needed to have her wits about her and be able to use every tool at her disposal. She pressed her lips into a firm line; hoping she could control her magic when the time came.

CHAPTER 5

Sorchia must have been suspicious because she arrived at dawn the next morning. Pierre had covered up the evidence of his tampering as best he could. Even so, Sorchia suspiciously examined the area. Pacing around the small tower until completely satisfied that nothing was amiss. Avella knew Pierre had hidden himself not far off; but still couldn't help holding her breath until Sorchia was satisfied there was nothing out of the ordinary tampering with her precious opportunity for revenge.

She climbed up nimbly, before filling Avella's water pitcher as usual. "Where's the bread, grandmother?" Avella asked hesitantly as she looked for the wrapped loaf her grandmother usually brought with her.

"I've decided you don't need any. It's not like you've done anything to deserve it yet." Sorchia raised a thin eyebrow, daring Avella to disagree.

Avella gulped, she knew if she were to have her chance to escape, she would need to play her cards just right. Now wasn't the time to let her emotions interfere. Letting the tears come, she threw her arms around the rigid woman.

"I'm sorry, grandmother." It wasn't hard to cry—not when she was this hungry. "Just give me time to get used to the idea." She withdrew from the embrace, slipping the tiny book out of her grandmother's pocket and into her own.

Sorchia stalked back to the window, her discomfort with the display of emotion showing as she pursed her lips in distaste. "I see that you've given it some thought. The next time I see you, I'll expect you to have an answer." She swung her leg over the windowsill.

Avella watched her climb to the bottom of the tower, fighting against the searing pain in her scalp. In her hand she clasped the book; it's worn cover tingling her hand with magic. The moment Sorchia's feet touched the ground, she made her move. With feverish hands, she pulled her hair inside the tower so Sorchia couldn't climb back up, then opened the book. Here's where the risk came in. Avella hadn't the foggiest idea of how to use Sorchia's precious book. Her hands shook as she flicked through the pages; she knew from observation the page Sorchia used was near the end of the book. Her eyes searched the pages, frantic to find something, anything that would help her. But it was all nonsense. Scrawls on ancient parchment. Tears came to her eyes as she realized her grandmother was going to win.

A howling shriek of anger interrupted. Avella glanced out the window to see her grandmother's face twisted in fury. "How dare you? You sneaky little thief. After everything I've done for you."

Grandmother raised her hands, opening her mouth to speak; but she was too late. Pierre appeared, and quick as a flash, tied her wrists and legs together.

"Put something in her mouth," Avella shouted down from the tower. She had given up on the idea of shrinking her hair back to its original length and instead was sawing it with the bread knife. A painful process, considering the thickness of her hair and the dullness of the knife. By the time she finished, grandmother was subdued, only muffled shrieks emerging from her mouth, which had Pierre's kerchief wrapped tightly around it.

"How will you get down? Should I go for rope" Pierre squinted up to the tower window.

Avella looked down at the shining pile of hair coiled on the floor. "I think I can do it." She tied one end around the leg of the bed and threw the rest out the window. Gripping it in both hands, she put one leg over the windowsill, gulping as she realized how high the tower really was. Forcing her eyes away from the ground below, she swung the other leg over. Then she was out, for one heart-stopping moment, dangling over the edge. Panic took over her, and she nearly fell to the ground. *Breathe,* she told herself. Pressing her feet against the wall, she climbed down, letting her legs collapse as they touched the ground below.

"Are you all right?" Pierre put a warm hand on her shoulder, his hazel eyes were kind and warm.

"Never better." Avella sat for a moment and let the sun kiss her skin. She threw a glance at her grandmother, still struggling on the ground.

"What are we going to do with grandmother?"

Sorchia glared at her, eyes full of poison.

"We'll let her stew for a while. We can send someone to untie her later. I'm sure people will be interested to know how she treats her granddaughter." He pressed his lips together in a firm line. He gave her one last disdainful glance, before he put his arm around Avella and led her into the forest.

"Is this yours?" Avella smiled in delight at the caravan. Robin's egg blue with yellow wheels it couldn't be a bigger contrast to the grim tower Avella had called home over the last few weeks. Two mules grazed nearby. Avella spotted a circle of stones with still glowing embers—a cooking fire.

"Yes. It's not fancy, but it's home for the time being." Pierre led Avella to the wooden steps leading into the small caravan. It was clean, tidy and cozy. A colorful quilt tucked into the bunk and cheerful curtains on the windows gave the caravan a homey touch.

"Come, sit." Pierre gestured to a single chair next to the potbellied stove. He sat on the edge of the bunk and stretched his legs out in front of him.

"I love it," Avella announced. And she did. Avella imagined the sheer freedom of a life on the road. The adventure of seeing different towns and villages; her mother had hated to travel; and when she did, it was a complicated and tense affair, fraught with complaints and nagging.

"You really like it?" Pierre's face lit up with pride. "But you're so..." he eyed her dingy, but obviously expensive dress.

"I do," Avella said, her voice firm and sure. "You can see the world. Go anywhere you want, do what you want to do...it must be amazing." She reached down to stroke Clover's soft ears. The dog pressed his head against her hand, soaking up the attention.

"I suppose," Pierre drew his brows together. "It gets lonely sometimes. Clover is good company, but he doesn't exactly have a lot to say. And I can't go *wherever* I want, I have a trade route to follow." He stood up, putting the kettle over the stove. "Tea? I even have biscuits for dipping."

"Yes, please." Avella put her hands over her stomach as it rumbled. Pierre rummaged in the store, producing ginger biscuits. Avella, delighted to drink something that didn't taste of Sorchia's bitter herbs, drank three cups, dipping the biscuits until they melted in her mouth. Pierre regaled Lucie with stories of his travel, which she absorbed wide-eyed, taking in every detail.

"I suppose we should leave soon if we want to reach town by nightfall... if that's where you want to go?" Pierre asked Avella.

"I suppose we should—I actually don't live in town, though. I live on the next estate." A dart of disappointment shot through Avella. Her mother and father would still be at court, and she could hardly return to her grandmother's house. She decided she would return home and wait for her mother and father. The housekeeper would still be there and it's not like her mother and father would notice she was back early anyway—not unless it impeded her mother's aspirations for social climbing. Avella cringed, knowing she would have some uncomfortable explanations to make if her mother discovered what happened at her grandmother's manor.

"Could I have a bath? I'm filthy." Avella couldn't show up to the manor looking like an unkempt scarecrow—not if she didn't want news of her premature return getting back to her mother.

"Of course. I usually just wash in the brook…" Pierre trailed off uncomfortably.

"The brook is fine," Avella answered quickly.

"I'll get some soap and a cloth. I might even have an extra tunic you can wear." Pierre disappeared into the back again. "I got a shipment of this," he stuck his head out holding a bar of wrapped soap.

Avella took the paper wrapped packet and opened it, breathing in the smell of bergamot and something else, something fresh, citrus, she thought, closing her eyes. "What is this one?" she re-wrapped the packet carefully.

"Bergamot and lemongrass?" Pierre poked his head out again, holding out a tunic and a soft pair of breeches. "I got the soap in my last trade shipment. Do you like it?"

"I don't want to take your things you're going to trade." Avella protested, trying to give back the package. She knew the more exotic scents would bring a good price at a market.

"Don't worry about it," Pierre waved away her argument. "I have plenty."

Avella took the bundle of clothes along with the soap, then followed Pierre. They went down a narrow path, coming to a brook rushing between the trees. Pebbles banked the rushing water. "It's not too deep, so I'll leave you to it." Faint pink tinged the tips of his ears as he turned away, leaving Avella to bathe in peace.

Avella undressed and stepped into the water, sucking in a breath as the shock of cold hit her. She quickly dipped her head in, her teeth chattering from the cold, and rubbed the soap into her hair, cringing at the dingy gray foam that floated downstream. After scrubbing her skin until it glowed pink, she stepped out again, shivering as she rubbed herself down briskly. She slipped the tunic over her head; it fell to her knees so she would need to find a belt later. She stepped into the breeches, rolling them up so they wouldn't drag on the ground. She sniffed at the clothes. They smelled fresh, like sunshine and warm grass. Bundling up her soiled dress, she headed back to the caravan.

It was then that she heard it. A cacophony of brays followed by a shout—Pierre. She froze, what was happening? Quickly pulling on her shoes, she rushed back to the clearing. There, a horrifying sight met her eyes. Her grandmother, malevolent fury glowing in her eyes, hair standing in every direction, with her arms raised, pointing toward the caravan. Dreadful sounds were coming out of her mouth—words. But not in any language Avella was familiar with. Surrounding her grandmother was a mass of seething vines and thorny branches, snaking and crawling across the ground. Branches with thorns the length of her hand.

They covered the small caravan coiling around it, leaving only a glimpse of robin's egg blue and the spoke of a yellow wheel showing through the thick growth. Her grandmother waved her hands, and the branches moved faster. They were tightening around the caravan, squeezing it. Avella heard the creak of wood straining under the pressure of the twisting vines.

Anger roared up from the bottom of Avella's soul. How could she? Pierre had been nothing but kind and generous to her. He didn't deserve this. Her heart pounded. Faster and faster. The effects of her grandmother's herbs had worn off, and Avella felt her magic welling up inside her, stronger than ever—nearly bursting out of her with its fury. The fire built up inside her, hot and fierce, and for once, she allowed it to flow, rushing through her veins. Crack! One of the thorny branches burst into a shower of flames. Then another, and another.

Sorchia turned, face distorted with rage. "How dare you?" she hissed. "You're as bad as your mother." She raised her hand, pointing at Avella, and a branch shot out, winding around her, the thorns dragging bloody scratches on her pale skin.

Avella didn't—couldn't—wouldn't stop. She stared at the branch immediately next to her grandmother. Boom! The earth shook as the branch exploded, catching the edge of her grandmother's dress on fire. Sorchia quickly beat it out, scorching her hands, but undeterred. Even as the smell of burnt flesh filled the air.

"Leave now," Avella was breathing hard. "Because I won't give up until you're gone." She flung a fiery dart past Sorchia's head. Sorchia's eyes widened as she realized what her granddaughter was capable of. She flung her arm up, sending a vine shooting out from underneath Avella's feet, grabbing her by the ankle and tumbling her to the ground with a thud.

She hit her head on one of the rocks that ringed the firepit, sending black spots swimming before her eyes. She fought to keep focused and scrambled to her feet, but another vine swept in, stabbing her in the side of the leg as it whipped around her, wrapping itself tight. The vine pinned Avella's arms o her side, rendering her helpless. She opened her eyes, Sorchia was leaning over her, a dark look of triumph in her eyes.

It's the end, Avella thought, as her grandmother stretched out her hand, gloating. A frantic barking sounded in her ears. Clover darted out from under the caravan and leapt on Sorchia, sinking his teeth into her thigh, making her stumble and miss. Avella took advantage of the opportunity by flinging one last ball of fire at Sorchia, this time grazing the side of her face. Sorchia fell to the ground, howling as she put her hand on the skin that was already red and bubbling.

"I won't hurt you unless I have to grandmother," Avella's voice was firm. "Now leave us alone and don't come back." She held out her hand, sending a crackling line of fire that landed at Sorchia's feet, sending her flying back another pace.

"Now go," she stared at the woman, determination etched in every feature.

Sorchia turned tail and ran, flying into the woods like a wraith. Avella stared after her until she had disappeared, then sank to the ground, exhausted.

"Pierre. Pierre?" Avella stood up slowly, she was under no illusion that her grandmother wouldn't return. And when Sorchia returned it would be with vengeance. The braying of the mules met her calls. They were nervous, showing the whites of their eyes, still frightened from the commotion. But Avella soon soothed them with soft words.

Avella circled the clearing, then dropped everything and ran. A crumpled heap lay at the side of the caravan. "Pierre?" she ran over, kneeling beside him. Deep scratches covered his skin, his clothes shredded and soaked with blood. She put a hand on his chest, relieved to feel the faint thud of his heartbeat under her hand.

Avella shook him, "Pierre. You have to wake up."

He groaned, rolling over, then opened his eyes.

"Can you stand?" Avella sagged under his weight as he struggled to sit up.

"My eyes. I think something's wrong with them." Avella looked at his face. A thorn had scraped both eyes.

"I'll get a cloth." With shaking hands, Avella dipped a cloth in some water and wrung it out before she laid it over his eyes.

"Do you think you can stand up?" Avella wiped his face with the cloth, catching her breath as she saw how pale his skin was underneath the blood.

"I think so." Pierre stood on shaky feet and let Avella guide him up the steps to the caravan. Avella had to move several of her grandmother's thorny branches out of the way, wincing when one of the jagged points caught the tender skin of her palm.

Pierre collapsed onto the bed. His breathing was heavy from the effort.

"Do you have salve?"

"I think so, in the box above the stove."

Avella lifted down the tin box over the stove, prying it open to reveal a neat row of labelled bottles, most of them for the animals she noticed, a roll of bandages and a flat metal container; that must be the salve. She opened it and the thick oily smell of herbs filled the small room. Using her fingers, she gently applied the thick yellow paste to the scratches, Pierre bit his lip once or twice, but let her treat him.

"What happened?" he asked as she screwed the lid back on the salve.

"She freed herself somehow, she must be able to control the plants even without the book. Avella sat on the edge of the bed. We fought her off, but it's only a matter of time until she comes back. I could have... gotten rid of her for good. I probably should have... but I just—couldn't," she confessed.

Pierre felt his way across the quilt and put his hand over Avella's. "That's what makes you different from her. You did the right thing. Unfortunately, I don't know how long she'll stay away—we can't stay here, it's too dangerous."

Avella worried her lip, Pierre's eyes had swelled up, the surrounding skin inflamed and hot. He needed medical attention. "Can you see at all?"

"Not yet. But I'm sure it will clear up." A ripple of apprehension ran through Avella's veins as Pierre attempted to put a brave face on the situation. Avella had little medical knowledge; but his eyes didn't look good.

"There's an apothecary in town, I know the healer there, she's one of the best; do you think the mules would let me drive them?" The threat of Sorchia's return hung heavy in the air; but she didn't want to bring it up again. Pierre had enough to worry about.

"Jewel will, Jingle—she's the dark brown one—she's a little feistier, but carrots are her weakness, if you give her a few she'll behave. I keep them in the basket under the caravan."

Avella nodded. The groom and the footman hitched up the carriage at the manor; but she'd watched enough that she should be able to figure it out. She had to. Leaving Pierre in the caravan, she made her way down the wooden steps. A few spiny branches, withered from the fire, wrapped themselves around the caravan. They were easy enough to remove; Avella dragged them to a pile at the edge of the clearing. Long scratches marred the paint, but everything still seemed to be in working order. Avella gave Jingle the carrots, and soon was fumbling with the tangle of harnesses, eventually getting the patient mules hitched to the cart.

Avella sat in the seat at the front of the caravan. She had never even driven a light carriage before. But how hard could it be? She picked up the reins and clucked in a firm voice. To her surprise, the mules moved, responding to her directions with ease. Avella followed the narrow track to the main road, and from there recognized familiar landmarks. Apparently, her grandmother's estate wasn't just close, it was directly adjacent to theirs. She mulled this over in her mind as the caravan rocked along; wondering how Natalie had kept her own mother a secret for so many years. Before she knew it, they arrived in the main square. It was market day, and the healer's apothecary was busy. Avella jumped down, leaving the mules in front of the apothecary, and pushed her way to the counter.

"Excuse me, is Althea here?" she asked the young girl serving the customers.

Althea bustled in from her mixing room, mortar and pestle still in hand. She smiled when she saw Avella.

"Avella? What happened to you? I thought you left for court with the rest of your family?"

"I'll tell you later." Avella had no desire to share details of her story in front of the many curious eyes turning her way. She was suddenly aware of her sooty tunic and wild hair.

"Yes, of course, dear." Althea suddenly noticed they were the center of attention. She ushered Avella into the back room and gestured to a tall wooden stool at the mixing table. Avella sat and looked around, breathing in the smell of the herbs and spices Althea used for her tinctures and poultices. A blazing fire in the hearth warmed the air. Althea moved to the fire, placing a kettle over the flames. "You look like you could use a good cup of tea."

Avella fidgeted with the edge of her tunic. "Yes, please, but first, I need your help with something. There's been an accident." She turned pleading eyes to Althea.

An expression of concern crossed Althea's face. "Your family? Are they all right?"

"As far as I know they're fine, still at court. I've been staying with my grandmother. Sorchia. Do you know her?"

Althea's eyes darkened as she pressed her lips together. "It's been a long time since I've heard that name spoken here."

"She's hurt someone... a friend. Can you come with me? He's in the caravan in front of your shop."

Althea led Avella out the side door and followed her to the caravan, ducking inside. Pierre lay on the bed, his eyes still closed. By now, every scratch had swelled, angry red lines radiated from the puffy skin.

"What happened to him?" Althea knelt by the bed, examining his face. He flinched, moaning when she touched his heated skin.

"My grandmother attacked him... with her thorns," Avella explained.

"If he's going to preserve his sight, we'll have to act now. And we need to keep this quiet. Just because we can't see her, doesn't mean her eyes and ears aren't everywhere. Bring the caravan around to the back of the apothecary, we'll use the private entrance."

Avella hurried outside, leading the mules to the back of the building, before she helped Pierre out of the caravan. By this time, he was delirious, stumbling as she guided him down the steps.

"Put him in here." Althea led her through her workroom to a small treatment room, no bigger than a cupboard. It contained a single bed, Avella helped Pierre to the bed, placing the pillow under his head.

"Can you see at all?" Althea began mixing some herbs, wrapping them in a cloth to make a poultice.

Pierre cracked his eyes open. "No, it hurts too much," he mumbled.

Althea lay the poultice on his eyes. "This should help, but we won't know for sure if we've saved his sight until morning. Your grandmother's poison is powerful, but I've been able to counteract it if I catch it early enough. Can you stay with him? I'll go take care of the mules."

Avella nodded, sitting on the edge of the bed, and taking Pierre's calloused hand in hers. It was hot and dry.

He moved his head back and forth, slurring incoherently.

"What was that?" Avella leaned closer. Was Pierre trying to tell her something.

"Book... book," he muttered.

Avella felt in her pocket. Her grandmother's book was still there, stinging her hand with a sudden jolt of magic.

"You think the book has the answer?"

He moved once, thrashing, then lay still, the poison in his system was too much for him.

With shaking hands, Avella took out the book, recoiling at the oily feeling seeping from its pages. Starting at the beginning, she paged through. The strange letters swam and danced before her eyes; always on the verge of making sense. She looked closer. There were strange pictures forming in the words. By now her hand was getting numb, the magic gathering, pooling in her blood until it was singing with the very intensity of it. Even so, the book was worthless if she couldn't use it.

"I wish I could help," Avella let the book fall to the floor. Tears of frustration welled up in her eyes, rolling down her cheeks and dripping onto the pillow beside him. A tear fell onto his face. She quickly wiped it away. To her surprise, the ravaged skin where the tear had fallen was healing. She stared in shock as she the red lines faded and shrank, leaving whole unblemished skin behind. Was this the answer? Avella quickly removed the compress. Collecting a tear in her finger, she touched it to his eye. The skin around his eye cleared. Instantly healthy, as if nothing had ever happened to it.

Althea bustled in, a small bowl of pungent brown paste in her hand. She stopped, stock still. "What happened to him?" she breathed, leaning in.

"I think…" Avella paused, knowing what she was about to say sounded crazy. "I think it was my tears." She touched another tear to the other eye, healing it as well.

"I've never seen anything like it before." Althea touched the skin on his cheek, where the redness had completely faded. Pierre lay—in a deep sleep now, no longer restless. "There's not even a scar. And the fever is gone as well." She searched Avella's face. "You did this?"

Avella nodded, biting her lip.

"What a wonderful gift," Althea laid a hand on the younger girl's head.

"I think—I think it came from the book."

Althea followed Avella, pointing at the book splayed out on the floor where she had dropped it.

"I see." Understanding dawned in Althea's eyes. "Your grandmother's book. Is that why she came after you?"

"Part of it. She wanted me to do something… and I couldn't do it," Avella lowered her lashes, golden brown hair falling across her face. Without a word, Althea wrapped the book in a cloth, avoiding direct contact. "This book is powerful and dangerous; you need to be very, very careful. If it gets into the wrong hands, it will end in disaster."

Avella took the wrapped package and returned the book to her pocket where it sat, burning her with its presence.

"What should I do?" she turned to Althea. "She came after me once and she'll do it again. I know she will."

"You'll need to go where she can't find you. I've known Sorchia for a while, and my mother knew her before I did. That woman is pure evil; she won't stop until she gets revenge."

"She can come with me." The two women jerked their heads. Pierre lay on the bed, wide awake, clear healthy eyes focused on Avella.

"You?" Avella asked incredulously.

The tips of Pierre's ears turned pink. "I'm going to Iasia, to start a shop there. You know they don't allow magic there. I don't have much to offer. But I'll need someone to help in the shop. Her grandmother won't find here in Lovan—Annecy is small, nothing more than a village. Even if she finds her, she won't be able to use her magic. You'll be safe."

Avella dropped her gaze.

"Is there something wrong?" Pierre fixed his hazel eyes on her.

"*I* have magic," Avella's voice was low. "Grandmother was giving me herbs to control it. Without the herbs, it would end in disaster—I couldn't do that." She flicked her eyes up to Pierre's.

"What kind of magic dear?" Althea's voice was gentle.

"Fire magic," Avella picked at a thread in the quilt.

"I think I can help." Althea closed the door, then lowered her voice to a whisper. "I would never do this in regular circumstances, but how would you feel about having your magic sealed?"

"Sealed?" Avella didn't know such a thing was possible. "It would be gone?"

"I believe your magic is part of you. Something to celebrate—not a shameful secret. But if you're in danger, this might be your only choice."

Tendrils of hope unfurled deep inside Avella's chest as a weight lifted off her shoulders. "Can you do that? Then Pierre wouldn't have to take me with him." A strange look crossed Pierre's face. Hurt? Avella pushed away her discomfort; after all, she was doing him a favor. He didn't need the burden. Not if he wanted to start a business in a new town. A town where tongues would already be wagging at the arrival of an outsider.

"It's difficult, but it is possible." Althea searched her eyes. "But, if I do this, seal your magic, it can't be easily unsealed. Are you sure you want to lock away this part of you?"

"Yes," Avella was firm. After all, what had her magic ever brought her besides destruction and heartache?

"Then, I'll prepare, we'll do it tonight."

CHAPTER 6

Althea lit a candle, chasing the evening shadows into the corners of her workroom. "Are you sure you want me to seal your magic?" she turned worried eyes to Avella.

Avella barked out a laugh, "I'm not just all right. I'm delighted. This is the part of me that's tormented me ever since it manifested. If my mother knew."

Pierre's face softened as he laid his hand on hers. They were sitting on stools pulled up to Althea's workbench. Althea's clients had left for the night, silence hung thick in the air; the doors locked and barred against curious villagers.

Althea sighed with a look of regret flashing in her eyes, "Close your eyes."

Obediently, Avella closed her eyes; breathing slowly in and out. Althea laid her warm hands on Avella's head. "This might feel strange, even painful. Take this and hold it tight when it becomes too much to bear."

Avella took the rolling pin Althea offered, wrapping her hands tight around the wooden dowel. "I'm ready."

Avella flinched—she felt that strange tingle again; pins and needles everywhere. They intensified, pouring over her in waves and burrowing under her skin until a fierce pain gripped every bone in her body. Then, as quickly as it came, it disappeared. Avella felt a hollow emptiness in her chest, nothing like the dull fog that Sorchia's herbs had induced. This was different, almost like a blank space opened up. She felt light, almost buoyant.

"Is it over?" Avella cracked her eyes open.

Althea nodded, exhaustion in every line of her face. She removed her hand from Avella's head.

"How do you feel?" Pierre asked.

"Different." Avella didn't know how to explain the strange hole that had opened up deep inside her.

"Are you ready to go back home?"

Avella stood up reluctantly, dreading the return to the cold, unfriendly manor. At least she wouldn't have to face her mother. It would be at least two days before a messenger reached the capital. Then she would have to pack up and make excuses for her hasty departure. At least a week before Avella would have to face Natalie's wrath.

Avella turned to embrace Althea as she stood in the doorway. "I don't know how I could ever thank you enough."

Althea smiled, "It was my pleasure, dear. And be careful, you're not out of danger yet; but soon your way will be clear." Her wise eyes held a mysterious warning. A warning Avella didn't understand. Althea clasped hands with Pierre, a knowing look passing between them before Althea turned away.

Avella turned to Pierre, "I'm ready." She set her jaw.

They were halfway back to the manor when they saw it. A strange glow, lighting up the night sky until it was a burnished red.

"Is that on your estate?" Pierre turned to Avella, worry clouding his face.

Avella nodded, "Maybe it's the hay. Sometimes they burn a patch so they can plant new." Even as she spoke, a lump of fear was heavy in her chest. Something was wrong. Very wrong.

As they turned down the lane, the sight that met Avella's eyes dashed every hope of a smooth homecoming. The manor house, Avella's childhood home, was lit up like a torch. The licking flames turned the sky red, ash raining down on them like black snow.

"Was anyone in the house?" Pierre jumped down and tied the mules to a tree. They were nervous, eyes rolling into the back of their heads at the billowing smoke and crackling flames.

Avella leapt after him. "The servants—I have to go help."

Pierre shouted after her, but she was already tearing down the drive as if possessed. Avella's family was safe in the castle. But the staff would have been asleep in their quarters at this time of night. The heat blasted against her. The house was now a wall of flames, higher than the trees.

She circled the house and ran behind the house, her breath ragged in her chest as the acrid smoke caught in her throat. Frantically, she peered through the whirling smoke. There. Through the ash and grit, human figures emerged, dazed and stumbling but alive. The housekeeper, butler, cook and other household staff. Singed in places, but whole and alive.

"What happened? Is everyone all right?" Avella stopped short, gasping for breath.

"We don't know... it was so sudden. One minute we were sleeping, the next moment we heard a bang. The whole place went up like tinder." Anton, the stable master, answered.

"The barn is safe and the wind is blowing in our favor. The horses are out of danger... but the house—we couldn't save it."

"Is there anyone still inside?" she had to shout over the roar of the fire.

"We accounted for everyone." It was Ann-Marie, the housekeeper, wrapped in her dressing gown, hair wild around her soot streaked face.

Fortunately, the stable was upwind from the fire and some distance from the main house, and with the help of Anton and Pierre, Avella herded everyone inside.

"You should sleep," Pierre put a blanket around Avella's shoulders. Avella clutched it around her shoulders. Her legs were numb with exhaustion. But she wouldn't, couldn't sleep until the fire died down and the danger passed.

"I can't believe she would do this to me—to us." She tipped her head up. "Is she really that filled with hate that she needed to destroy an entire family?"

Pierre guided her to a seat on a hay bale. "I don't know. What I do know is you're going to be in danger as long as your grandmother is alive."

Avella sat quietly, the realization that her grandmother would never stop her quest for revenge dawned on her. She clutched the blanket tight around *her* shoulders as she turned to Pierre, "When are you leaving for Lovan? If the offer's still open, I'll come."

His eyes searched hers, warm and kind. "I am, if you're sure you want to come with me," he brushed a strand of her golden hair over her shoulder.

"It's the only way."

"But what about your family? Don't you want to tell them where you're going?"

Avella laughed, "My family—my mother—was the one who sent me to Sorchia. All Natalie cares about is her position at court and how high she can climb. When they find out about the fire, they'll hate me more than ever."

"Let's go then," Pierre held out his hand, and Avella took it.

CHAPTER 7

Avella lifted her face to the sunshine as the caravan bounced along the rutted road. It was two days since they left the smouldering ruins of the manor behind. In the morning they would cross the Lovanian border; and Avella couldn't wait.

"Do you want to stop in town?" Pierre asked, turning toward her.

"Can we? Is it safe?" Avella was still wearing Pierre's old tunic. Although never one for frills and fripperies, it would be nice to wear something that fit.

"Of course." More village than town, it consisted of a tavern, and a few shops strung along the single street. But it was market day, the square was filled with venders. Avella browsed the stalls, choosing a few lengths of fabrics she could fashion into simple dresses. Her boots would do until she could get to a proper shoemaker.

"Did you find anything?" Pierre found her poking through a tray of silver hairpins. He handed her a few skewers of dough covered in sugar attached to the ends.

"Delicious," Avella brushed crumbs of sugar from around her mouth.

Pierre laughed, "I love those, too, I get them every time I come through this town."

Avella wiped her hands on her tunic and chose two silver hairpins. She had been using a bit of twine to tie her hair back. It would be nice to look presentable.

"I found someone at the tavern, they're going to the capital. Do you want to send a message to your mother and father?"

Apprehension lanced through Avella's chest. "Do you think they'll be able to find me?" she turned her anxious gaze toward Pierre.

"He'll be discreet. If it makes you feel better, we'll ask him to leave the message at the gate, they'll never know who brought it."

Avella nodded with troubled eyes, "I guess we could do that."

The tavern keeper brought her parchment and a pen and Avella sat down to write, pausing frequently to gather her thoughts. She finished with a sigh, folding the parchment carefully and handing it to Pierre when she finished.

Avella left the village with a sense of relief. The next morning, she would be in Lovan. Safe and anonymous. None of the pressures of court, marrying up, or pleasing her difficult mother.

That evening they stopped for the night in a clearing near the road. Avella cooked, she wasn't good at it, but her lonely childhood had forced her to spend many hours in the kitchen, and she was getting better. Pierre had no shortage of spices or seasonings stored in the back of the caravan and enjoyed her experiments, insisting every one of them was delicious.

Tonight, was beef stew, Pierre brought the meat, along with the vegetables from the market. Avella stirred the pot over the fire, breathing in the rich scent.

"What do you think?" she held the spoon out to Pierre.

"Delicious," Pierre's nose twitched. "Did you put some pepper in there?"

"Yes, is it too much?" Avella took a bite, then coughed, her eyes watering. "That's terrible. You can't eat that." Her face fell. She had been hoping to show him how useful she could be.

"It's fine," Pierre insisted. "But maybe just a pinch less pepper next time?" He tweaked her nose.

That night they ate bread and dried meat for supper. The stew proved inedible, even Clover turned up his nose when they offered it to him; much to Avella's dismay. Stomach full, Avella yawned. All the fresh air made her sleepy at night.

"Go on to bed. We have another long day tomorrow." Pierre had insisted that Avella sleep in the caravan; he slept on a bedroll by the fire at night; putting up a shelter if it rained.

Avella crawled under the quilt on the narrow bed, falling asleep as soon as her head hit the pillow.

A muffled shout followed by frantic barking woke her, along with the sounds of struggle. She bolted up in the bed, holding her breath. Snatching up the poker, she tiptoed to the window; peering through the gap in the curtains. There were three of them. Bandits by the look of them. Big burly men. One of them was on top of Pierre struggling, nearly rolling him into the fire. The other bandit grabbed Jingle by the halter. Clover had the remaining bandit occupied, barking and growling as the bandit fended him off with one of the sticks from the fire.

Avella knew she would have to act fast. The only thing on Avella's side was the element of surprise. Cursing herself for being so quick to seal her magic, she moved soundlessly to the door. She opened it slowly. The bandits weren't expecting anyone to be inside the caravan. With a shout, she leaped down the steps, brandishing the poker. She sliced it at the bandit who had Pierre in a chokehold. The poker clanged against the side of the bandit's head. He howled, loosening his grip enough to give Pierre a chance to elbow him in the gut and slide out of his grip.

Avella waved the poker again, cracking one of the bandits on the side of his chest. He howled, clutching his ribs, and staggered away. Avella turned her attention to the other bandit who had sent Clover whimpering under the caravan. But he was too quick for her. He grabbed the poker, wrenching it out of her hands. Avella scampered back, searching the area for something else she could defend herself with.

"I've got it. Let's go," still clutching the poker, the bandit ran to join his companion; melting into the dark forest.

"Are they gone?" Avella sat on the ground, breathing hard.

"I think so," Pierre put a cautious hand to the swelling lump on his head.

"I wonder why they left so quickly." Clover came skulking out from his hiding place under the caravan. He put his head in Avella's hand, letting her scratch him behind his ears.

Pierre pressed his lips together, "I think it's because they got what they came for." He went to the back of the caravan; where he stored his goods. Avella trailed behind him. She knew by his expression this wasn't good. The back door of the caravan hung open, creaking in the breeze. They had ransacked his store. Pierre swung inside, taking out a few boxes; before he turned to Katherine; an expression of utter dismay on his face.

"They found it." His eyes were dark.

"Found what?" Katherine looked up at him, heart sinking.

"The gold. I'd been saving to open a shop. I kept it with the spices. They must have known where to look; I don't know *how*. I was always so careful to keep it hidden." He sat on the edge of the caravan, a defeated expression on his face. "It took years to save that up."

Katherine put a tentative hand to his shoulder. "How much gold do you need?" she knew she would need to tread carefully. Pierre was far too self-reliant to accept a handout.

"Enough to buy a cottage... a shop in the village; maybe even some of land as well."

"I have gold... I could loan you some; in exchange for your help."

Pierre turned to her. "What do you need help with?"

"Shelter, protection. I'll need to support myself when I get to Annecy. We could open the shop together; you have all the expertise." She held her breath, hoping she hadn't offended him.

"I suppose that could work," Pierre said, his voice thoughtful. "Are you sure? It's not too late to live in the city."

"I do. I like small towns. And I don't want people to get suspicious—you know how gossip travels. I'll have to have some sort of trade. And you've done so much for me already. I can read and write, my mother made sure I got an education. I could do the accounts; that sort of thing. I know very little about the buying and selling; but I could learn."

"Don't worry, I can teach you," Pierre turned to Avella, his eyes dark.

"Good." Avella scrambled past him, darting inside the caravan. After a few minutes of rustling, she emerged, holding a small canvas sack. She handed it to Pierre. He untied the drawstring and looked inside.

"Where did you get this?" he reached inside, it was full of heavy gold coins.

"I brought it with me, from the estate. I figured if I was leaving, I should take some of my inheritance with me." Avella grinned. "Will it be enough for a shop—a cottage?"

Pierre brought out a handful of the gold pieces. "You could get five cottages with this gold. We'll have the finest shop in the county."

EPILOGUE

Avella rocked her daughter Lucie in her arms. The third of many, she hoped. Little Katherine sat by the fireplace playing with her doll, and Marion, always the serious one, read a book. Life was good to Pierre and Avella. The people of Annecy had welcomed them with open arms; they surprised no one when they married a few months after arriving into town.

Trade was good. So good Pierre had expanded to three lines of caravans. He traded up and down Lovan and Iaisia. He built Avella and the girls a big stone house on the main street; not a manor—but Avella preferred it that way. Avella seldom thought of the life she had left behind. Her husband and daughters engrossed her so.

Although Avella kept her grandmother's little book. Usually it gathered dust on the shelf; but from time to time, she brought it out, fingering it—wondering at the power it had held over her grandmother. Now, it sat on the little shelf next to her, its worn spine and threadbare pages standing out against the shiny new books that lined the shelves. Avella looked away. There was no point dwelling on the past now. She had a life—a good life.

A knock at the door interrupted her thoughts. Who would knock on the door at this time of the night? She wondered; Pierre was traveling on business with the caravans; he wouldn't be back for days. She set Lucie in her little cot and went to open the door. Her mouth opened in shock.

"Althea?"

She stepped back, letting Althea come in out of the cold. Althea brushed the rain off her shoulders and took a seat by the fire.

"What brings you here?" The servants had left for the night, so Avella bustled about, getting tea ready. She laid out a plate of tarts on the side table along with cream and sugar.

"I came to bring you news," Althea stirred the cream and sugar into her the china cup.

"Your grandmother, she's dead."

"How did it happen?" Avella sat down with a thump. The words sounded hollow in her ears.

"The fever came to our part Iaisa. Most recovered; but she did not." Althea warmed her hands around her cup. Avella looked at her closely. She was older now, slower, her hair now threaded with silver.

"And what of the family—my father, Madelaine, mother?" The words caught in Avella's throat.

"They rebuilt the manor. Your sister...didn't marry the prince. Which is good judging from what I hear of his character."

Avella nodded. She knew of the royal family of Iasia. The prince welcomed a daughter the year Katherine was born. The entire town was buzzing for weeks with the news of a marriage alliance between her and Frederich, the young prince of Lovan.

"Did she marry anyone?"

"No," Althea's eyes tightened, her mouth drew into a thin line.

"When your family came back; there was an accident—involving your grandmother. It left your sister disfigured."

Avella's cup stopped halfway to her mouth.

"She's a very angry woman who needs someone to blame. I know what happened was not your fault. It was your grandmother's doing, seeking revenge. Madelaine blames you for the accident."

Avella set the cup down with a jolt. She glanced down at Lucie, still sleeping in her cot. The dark lashes lay across the rosy cheeks like silk as she dreamed.

"Does Madelaine know where I am?"

"She doesn't... they only know you ran away. I alone knew the truth of where you went. I kept in touch with Pierre." Althea stared at the fireplace, searching for the right words to say. "Unfortunately, she was there when Pierre came through town one day. Someone recognized him, one of the staff from the manor. She doesn't know where you are; and she doesn't know you and Pierre are still together; but she knows you're in Lovan. She's been sending people to search for you."

"Does she know about the girls?" Avella lowered her voice as she gave Katherine and Marion a sidelong glance.

"No. Pierre knew better. I don't think he even spoke to them; just passed them in the street. He came to me right after—he explained how to find you. I came straight here; Pierre's on his way, but he didn't want anyone to follow him; it might delay him a while."

Avella caught her breath, her mind spinning. She knew she had to protect her daughters and Pierre. But how? She bit her lip, knowing deep in her heart, there was only one answer. If she were gone, her daughters would be safe.

"I'm going to need your help," she turned to Althea, who nodded in understanding. Then, her eyes swimming in tears. She pressed a kiss to Lucie's downy head; wondering if this would be the last time that she would hold her precious child. Then she rose from her seat and went to prepare.

Find out what happens next in the Crown and the Sceptre series in *Brave – A Fairy Tale Retelling of Beauty and the Beast.*

BOOKS IN CROWN AND SCEPTRE SERIES SERIES

Free – A Fairy Tale Retelling of Rapunzel (Novella)
Brave – A Fairy Tale Retelling of Beauty and the Beast (coming soon)
Strong – A Fairy Tale Retelling of the Princess and the Pea (coming soon)
True – A Fairy Tale Retelling of Puss in Boots (coming soon)
Loyal – A Fairy Tale Retelling of Red Riding Hood (coming soon)
Pretty - A Fairy Tale Retelling of the Princess Frog (coming soon)
Valor - A Fairy Tale Retelling of Jack and the Beanstalk (coming soon)

Don't miss out!

Visit the website below and you can sign up to receive emails whenever Kristina J Jordan publishes a new book. There's no charge and no obligation.

https://books2read.com/r/B-A-KPEO-KLMPB

BOOKS 2 READ

Connecting independent readers to independent writers.